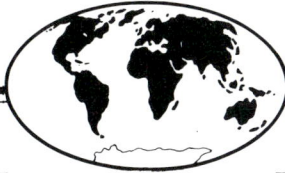

WORLD IN VIEW

CUBA

Emily Morris

STECK-VAUGHN
LIBRARY
Austin, Texas

Library of Congress Cataloging-in-Publication Data

Morris, Emily.
   Cuba / Emily Morris.
     p.   cm.—(World in view)
   Includes index.
   Summary: Surveys the history, culture, people, lifestyles,
trade and development, and future of Cuba.
   ISBN 0-8114-2439-1
   1. Cuba—Juvenile literature. [1. Cuba.] I. Title.
II. Series.
F1758.5.M67   1991   90-10354
972.91—dc20   CIP AC

Designed by Julian Holland Publishing Ltd
Picture research by Jennifer Johnson
Consultant: Bruce Taylor, Ph.D., University of Dayton

Cover: *Trinidad de Cuba and the sea.*
Title Page: *Cubans dressed up for a carnival.*

Typeset by Multifacit Graphics, Keyport, NJ
Printed and bound in the United States
  2 3 4 5 6 7 8 9 0 LB 95 94 93 92

Photographic credits
Cover: ©Paolo Gori/The Image Bank
title page: Michael Macintyre/Hutchison Library, 5 Liba Taylor/Select, 8, 9, 10, 12 Christine
Pemberton/Hutchison Library, 17, 21, 23 Mary Evans Picture Library, 26, 29 Lyn Smith, 30 Nicola
Seyd, 31 Mansell Collection, 33, 36 Nicola Seyd, 39 Christine Pemberton/Hutchison Library, 44 Julio
Etchart, 45 Christine Pemberton/Hutchison Library, 47 Julio Etchart, 48 Liba Taylor/Select, 51, 52
Lyn Smith, 53 Liba Taylor/Select, 56 Lyn Smith, 57 Liba Taylor/Select, 60 Christine Pemberton/
Hutchison Library, 61 Lyn Smith, 66 Emily Morris, 68 Liba Taylor/Select, 69 Christine Pemberton/
Hutchison Library, 72 Emily Morris, 74 Lyn Smith, 76 Liba Taylor/Select, 77 Emily Morris, 80 Lyn
Smith, 81 Liba Taylor/Select, 85 Julio Etchart, 86 Felix Greene/Hutchison Library, 89 Liba Taylor/
Select, 91 Michael Macintyre/Hutchison Library, 92 Emily Morris, 93 Julio Etchart.

Contents

CUBA

U.S.
(Florida)

Gulf of
Mexico

ATLANTIC
OCEAN

N

Straits of Florida

B
A
H
A
M
A
S

Great Bahama Bank

Tropic of Cancer

Cay Sal Bank
(Bahamas)

Nicholas Channel

Santaren Channel

Habana (Havana)

Archipiélago de Sabana

C

Colón

Sierra los
Órganos

Sierra del
Rosario

Batabano
Gulf

Archipiélago de Camagüey

Yucatan Channel

Archipiélago
de los
Canarreos

Habana

U

San Juan
(4,792 ft.)

Morón

B de
Cochinos
(Bay of Pigs)

Moa R.

B

Cauto R.

San Pedro R.

Cibreras R.

A

Salado R.

MEXICO

Isla de la Juventud
(Isle of Youth)

Cayo
Largo

G
r
e
a
t
e
r

Archipiélago
de los Jardines

Guacanayabo
Gulf

Yoa R.

Guantanamo
Bay

Windward
Passage

Grand Cayman
(UK)

A
n
t
i
l
l
e
s

Sierra Maestra
(7,225 ft.)

C
a
y
m
a
n

T
r
e
n
c
h

JAMAICA

HAITI/DOMINICAN
REPUBLIC

CARIBBEAN
SEA

0   100 miles

0   100 kilometers

The Cuban flag

1 Introducing Cuba

Cuba is the largest island in the Caribbean Sea. The island lies at the mouth of the Gulf of Mexico, where the Caribbean Sea meets the Atlantic Ocean, off the coast of Central America. Its neighbors are Jamaica to the south and Haiti to the east, both 50 miles (80 kilometers) away. Florida, in the United States of America, is 90 miles (145 kilometers) to the north, and Mexico's Yucatan Peninsula lies the same distance to the west. This central position, between the United States, the Caribbean, and Central America has attracted the interest of surrounding countries over the centuries.

The main road from the town of Trinidad into the Sancti Spiritus Highlands carries little traffic. These beautiful, heavily forested mountains have few people living in them.

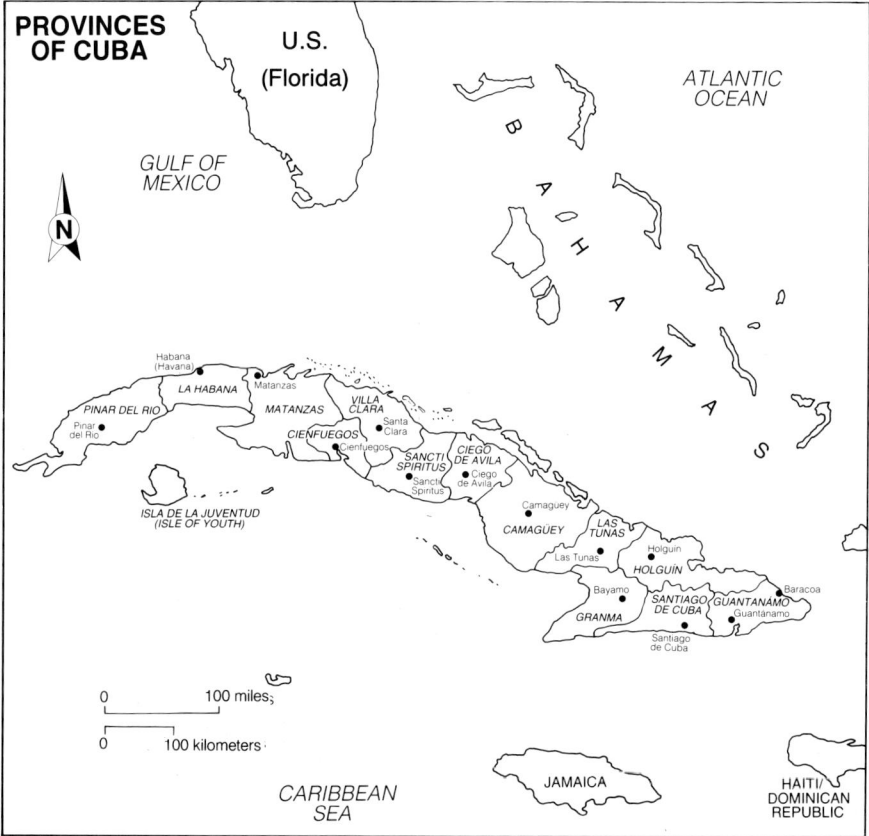

PROVINCES OF CUBA

U.S.
(Florida)

ATLANTIC
OCEAN

GULF OF
MEXICO

N

B A H A M A S

Habana
(Havana)
LA HABANA
Matanzas
PINAR DEL RIO
MATANZAS
VILLA
CLARA
Santa
Clara
Pinar
del Rio
CIENFUEGOS
Cienfuegos
SANCTI
SPIRITUS
CIEGO
DE AVILA
Ciego
de Avila
Sancti
Spiritus
ISLA DE LA JUVENTUD
(ISLE OF YOUTH)
Camaguey
CAMAGÜEY
LAS
TUNAS
Holguin
Las Tunas
HOLGUIN
Baracoa
Bayamo
SANTIAGO
DE CUBA
GUANTANAMO
Guantánamo
GRANMA
Santiago
de Cuba

0   100 miles
0   100 kilometers

CARIBBEAN
SEA

JAMAICA

HAITI/
DOMINICAN
REPUBLIC

6

The island of Cuba is divided into 14 provinces, plus the special self-governing district or municipality of the Isle of Youth. Each province is governed by a provincial assembly. The members of this assembly are elected by members of the island's 167 municipal assemblies, who are elected by the people every two and a half years. National laws and policy decisions are voted on by the National Assembly, whose members are elected by the provincial assemblies every five years. The president is elected by the National Assembly every five years. Since 1959, Fidel Castro has been president. He is also the chairman of the only political party, the Communist Party of Cuba.

Cuba's shape resembles the shape of an alligator, reaching 745 miles (1,200 kilometers) from the tip of its tail in the west to the end of its nose in the east, but with an average width of only 60 miles (95 kilometers). About 60 percent of the land is low-lying and flat, with plains, swamps, and gentle slopes. The rest is hills and mountains. The highest and most rugged mountain range is the Sierra Maestra, at the eastern end of Cuba. These mountains reach a height of nearly 6,500 feet (2,000 meters) above sea level. Other mountain ranges are the Trinidad-Sancti Spiritus Highlands in the center of the island and the Sierra de Los Organos in the north. The Republic of Cuba includes over 1,000 small islands. The largest is the Isle of Youth, 380 square miles (990 square kilometers). The smallest islands are just a few yards across.

Cayo Largo is one of 1,000 islands that surround Cuba. It is one of the islands that form the archipelago belonging to the Isle of Youth. The jetties around the coast are used by local fishermen and tourists.

Climate and vegetation

There is plenty of sunshine in Cuba, on average eight hours a day. There are two seasons: the dry winter season, from November to early May, and the rainy summer season, from mid-May to October. However, even in the dry season it rains at least once a month. The average temperature is 77°F (25°C) which is hot but not scorching, although temperatures can sometimes reach 90°F (32°C) in the summer. There is no danger of frost, because the lowest temperature is 46°F. The main natural hazard for trees is the danger of hurricanes, which sometimes come at the end of summer, in September and October, with torrential rain and strong winds. Cubans have experienced more than 50 storms of hurricane intensity this century.

Cuba's subtropical climate provides perfect climatic conditions for lush vegetation. When Christopher Columbus first saw Cuba in 1492, he noted:

The verdant greenery reaches almost down to the water . . . trees all along the river, beautiful and green . . . with flowers and fruits each according to their kind, and with countless little birds singing very sweetly . . . That island is the most beautiful that eyes have ever seen.

The land he saw was covered with tropical rain forest. The forest had many hardwoods, such as mahogany and teak, which have been used to build ships, houses, and carved furniture. In the tropical forest grew a wide selection of native plants, many of which produced fruit such as

A farmer hangs bunches of tobacco leaves on one of the many drying racks scattered around the countryside of the province of Pinar del Rio. The cultivated tobacco fields are broken up by groups of the tall Royal palm, Cuba's national symbol.

The Valley of Viñales was once covered in lush subtropical forest. The forest still survives on the steep hills that surround the valley floor, but most of the flat land is now covered by small farms and only small areas of woodland are left.

plantain, which is similar to the banana, wild fig, mango, guava, papaya, prickly pear, and pineapple. The native people lived on these fruits, and also ate the fish they caught from the rivers and ocean.

Much of the tropical rain forest that Columbus saw is now gone. As farmers started to grow crops for export, they cleared the forest from the land that they wanted to use for cultivation. Now, most of the forest that remains is in the mountain areas. National parks have been created to protect the forest, and in some areas conservationists are starting to replant trees.

Wildlife
On dry land, small mammals and reptiles are plentiful. There are many types of squirrels, rats, and mice that are native to Cuba, including the *almiqui*, a type of shrew and the world's smallest mammal. The larger mammals that can now be found, such as cattle and horses, were introduced by the Spanish. Cuba also boasts the smallest frog and smallest scorpion in the world, along with many other reptiles such as newts and lizards, iguanas and chameleons. Although there are no poisonous snakes, the largest at 13 feet (4 meters) long, can look very frightening.

In the rivers, coastal marshes, and mangrove swamps, there are many alligators and crocodiles to be wary of. They have been hunted for their skins, but now they are carefully farmed and the killing is controlled, to make sure that they survive. Near the coast, there are a startling number of large land crabs with huge claws, which can run sideways very fast.

Swimmers in the oceans should beware of stinging jellyfish. However, it is easy to forget this slight danger when exploring the miles of beautiful corals, or watching the brightly colored small fish that live in the shallow coastal waters. Names such as the parrot fish, peacock fish, butterfly fish, and zebra fish give some idea of their coloring. Lobsters, squid, octopus, mussels,

11

Iguanas live in large numbers on some of the islands around Cuba. They feed on the scrubby island vegetation and are strong swimmers. Most of the dozen iguanas in this picture are fully grown.

crabs, sponges, and oysters are also abundant.

Tortoises and turtles used to be killed for their meat and shells, but now they are protected. In the deeper waters, dolphins, swordfish, sawfish, and barracudas swim.

Birds and flowers

The forests teem with brightly colored parrots. Even more dramatic are the large pink flamingos that live in the shallow waters of the coast. At the other end of the scale is the bee hummingbird, known locally as *zun zun*, the smallest bird in the world. In the countryside, the bird which can always be seen, circling high in the sky or resting on telegraph wires, is the Aura vulture. Its slow, lazy flight contrasts with the quick, busy common sparrow, which is ever-present, in town and countryside. For hunting, the Spanish introduced the pheasant, quail, and guinea fowl, which have learned to live in the wild.

The bright tropical flowers attract 180 species of butterflies and moths, 28 of which are found in Cuba and nowhere else in the world.

For many centuries, the island people had lived among this natural wealth, but had been satisfied to take only what they needed, and to leave nature otherwise undisturbed. The European explorers were different. Columbus noted in his diaries: "It is certain that where there is such marvelous scenery, there must be much from which profit can be made." He was right.

2 Spain's "Ever-faithful Isle"

The Cuban people speak Spanish, and there are many Spanish influences in the buildings, music, and culture. This is because Cuba was ruled by Spain for nearly four centuries. However, the visitor will quickly notice that there are other influences on the life and culture of the Cubans. Most importantly, there is a great influence from the Africans who were first brought to Cuba to work for the Spanish as slaves. Today, the Cuban people are described as a cultural mix from Africa and Spain. There are also some people who are descended from Chinese workers, and other Europeans and Latin Americans who came to Cuba looking for work. All these people have equal rights in Cuba, and together they enjoy the richness of a combined culture.

Before the Spanish sailors arrived, Cuba had its own civilization. There were three different societies who lived in different parts of the country: the Guanahatabey, the Ciboneys, and the Tainos. The Guanahatabey people came from Mexico. They lived in caves and used stones as tools. Some of the cave drawings they did can still be seen today. They show events in their lives, magical signs, and charts of the stars and planets. Archaeologists have examined some of the cave drawings and remains, and have estimated that the Guanahatabey arrived about 5,500 years ago.

When the next wave of visitors arrived in boats, the Guanahatabeys moved out of the center of the island. Newcomers called the Ciboneys came from the southern part of North America. They were followed by the Taino people who had traveled to Cuba from South America. They lived in huts, and had a very different way of life from the Guanahatabeys. Although there may have been some conflict between these different peoples at first, they settled down peacefully, following their own way of life.

Until 1492, the Cubans had no idea that there was any other land to the east beyond the islands of the Caribbean Sea. Meanwhile, the Europeans on the eastern side of the Atlantic Ocean believed that across the sea to the west there was only the edge of the world.

When Christopher Columbus set sail from Spain to find out what was beyond the sea, people thought he was crazy, and said that he would fall off the edge of the world. After eight weeks at sea, even his own sailors started to believe that they would never see land again, and wanted to go back home before it was too late. However, Columbus persuaded them to continue, and at last they sighted land. First they found an island in what we now know as the Bahamas. The second place they landed, in October 1492, was Cuba.

Columbus and his sailors believed at first that they had sailed all the way around the world to India, and so they called the people they found "Indians." When Columbus looked around the island, he was very impressed. He felt that Cuba would be a valuable possession for the king of Spain. However, it was not until nearly 20 years later, in 1510, that the Spanish king sent Diego

Velazquez, with 300 men, to claim Cuba for Spain. Within the following five years, the Spanish built eight settlements. One of these was later to become Havana, which is now the island's capital city.

The gold seekers

The early years of Spanish settlement were violent. The Spanish were only interested in finding gold and other precious articles, which would make them, and Spain, rich and powerful. They were not interested in learning about the way of life of the people they found there, or in trading with them.

When they started to settle, the Spanish declared that they owned the land and the people who lived on it. They started to use the Indians as slaves. If the Indians resisted, the Spanish would murder whole villages. Sometimes they even hunted Indians, like animals, for sport. Many of those who survived fled to the mountains, where they starved. If they were recaptured they would be punished and enslaved. Some of those slaves were kept to work for the settlers, and others were sent back to Spain to be sold to rich people there.

By the time the Indians realized what was happening, it was too late. They were slow to rally to defend themselves against the invaders, because they lived in such small communities, each with their separate ruler. Also, the Spanish had guns, against which the Indian's knives and arrows were almost useless.

There was one famous Indian chief who, with his wife, tried to organize a rebellion against the

When the Spanish conquistadores *arrived in Cuba they captured the native Indians and used them as slaves to dig for gold. The Indians were treated very harshly and many of them died.*

Spanish. His name was Hatuey, and he and his wife were captured in the south of Cuba. After seeing his people murdered, he was burned at the stake in 1512. Before they burned him, the Spanish offered him the chance to accept their Catholic religion, with the promise that if he did, he would go to heaven instead of hell after his death. His answer, recorded by a Spanish assistant, who witnessed the event, was "If torture and murder are the wishes of your God, I cannot be part of that religion and I cannot see myself enjoying heaven with such men who obey

17

Slavery

The Spanish settlers started to make a living from farming but, with nearly all the Indians dead, they found that there were not enough people to do the work. The settlers had been given land and paid by the Spanish government to settle in the new colony, and had had an easy life, using the Indians to do all the physical work. They had no intention of doing that work themselves.

At first, the Spanish government started to send convicts from Spain to Cuba to work as slaves in the fields and the mines. Then they found that traders had acquired people from leaders along the coasts of Africa, and were offering them for sale as slaves.

The slave traders treated their captives very cruelly. It has been estimated that in the 400 years of slavery, 60 million African people, usually the youngest and fittest, were secured by the slave traders. Some 50 million died before arriving in the Americas, while the other ten million faced unbearable hardship. Many slaves tried to escape, but they were hunted down by the slave owners' dogs. Death was the punishment for helping a runaway slave. From the earliest days of slavery, the slaves tried to revolt, but the first major, organized slave uprising in Cuba was not until 1823.

In 1845, Britain led an international effort against the slave trade, but this was not accepted by the Spanish in Cuba. The slaves increased their efforts to gain their freedom and, in 1849, there was another uprising of the slaves against their owners. For the first time this uprising spread throughout the whole country. Finally in 1886 Cuba was the last island in the Caribbean to make slavery illegal.

the cruel wishes of such a God. Are there any Spaniards in Paradise? . . . In which case I have no wish to be seen there myself."

Indian massacres

Of course, not all the Spanish were in favor of this cruelty, though many accepted it because they believed that Indians were inferior beings. One person who tried to protect the Indians was a bishop, Bartolomé de las Casas. He said that with his own eyes he had seen the Indians suffer worse atrocities and cruel treatment than anyone could ever imagine. In 1542, he succeeded in getting a law passed in Spain to protect the Indians and to make it illegal to use them as slaves. However, the following year, after pressure from the Spanish settlers, the law was withdrawn.

By 1620, as a result of the Spanish conquest nearly all the native people had died. The ones who survived the slaughter and diseases became slaves and were sent down into dangerous gold mines, used to work in the cotton fields, or forced to dive for pearls. The slaves were worked so hard and fed so little that they died of overwork and malnutrition. There is no record of the language that the Indians spoke, except for a few words that were adopted by the Spanish that survive today, such as *hamoc* (hammock), *tabac*, *sikar* (cigar), *canoe*, *potato*, and *barbeque*. All these are things that the Spanish had not seen before, and that were eventually brought over to Europe. Both Cuba and Jamaica got their names from the Indian language, from the words for "center of the island" (*cubanacan*) and "the isle of woods and water" (*xayamaca*).

During the same period, the Spanish had also used up nearly all the gold mines in Cuba and many returned to Spain or moved on to find gold in Mexico and Peru. The king of Spain declared that if the Spanish settlers left Cuba they would be put to death, but the promise of gold was more powerful than the fear of punishment. Only a few remained, trying to make a living out of mines dug for profitable metals, including copper and nickel. Some eventually turned to growing crops to sell such as cocoa, coffee, indigo plants, tobacco, and sugar. By the middle of the sixteenth century, Cuba had become emptier than it had been for thousands of years. Although it was still a beautiful island, it was no longer attractive to Europeans. For a few decades, Cuba was forgotten—until another use was found for it, as a shelter for Spanish ships.

Two centuries of piracy

Although the gold in Cuba had run out, the Spanish had now discovered huge amounts of gold and jewels in Central and South America, especially in the Aztec and Inca empires of Mexico and Peru. The sailing ships that were laden with all this treasure had a very dangerous journey across the sea, to take their cargo back to Spain. They had to face the terrible natural dangers of hurricanes and storms, shallows and reefs, and also the danger of pirates. The heavily laden treasure ships from the mainland could stop in Cuba, to shelter from hurricanes or to gather into a convoy for protection against pirates, before setting off for the long journey home. As a result, Cuba's ports of Havana and

Santiago de Cuba gained importance. Some of the pirates raided the ships to make money for themselves. They smuggled stolen goods into other countries. Others were doing it to take treasure back to their king or queen. Wars were fought on the high seas between the navies of England, Spain, France, Holland, and Portugal. Besides attacking the ships, the pirates attacked the ports, which had become wealthy as trading posts because of the treasure trade. Some towns, like Havana and Santiago, built strong fortifications as protection from these raids.

Eventually, by the second half of the eighteenth century, it had become harder for pirates to make a living because the gold was running out and the convoys and cities had become so well protected. Gradually, some of the pirates became either smugglers or gun-runners, or joined the navy.

There were many famous pirate captains like "Blackbeard" and François le Clerc or "Peg Leg." British pirates such as Henry Morgan or Sir John Hawkins were among the fiercest. There were also female pirates such as Anne Bonney and Mary Read (shown here) who struck fear into the hearts of many sailors.

Some retired and many went back to their native countries, but some remained in Cuba, settling where they had once raided.

Fight for independence

In Cuba all the laws came from Spain, and all exchange of goods was controlled by Spain. The prices paid by the Spanish were lower than the prices that other buyers were willing to pay, so the Cubans resented this law. They also saw that the Spanish government was making great profits by reselling Cuban tobacco and sugar to other customers.

At first, many Cubans showed their dissatisfaction simply by trading sugar or tobacco illegally with foreign buyers. However, the risks of this smuggling were high and the penalties were harsh.

Eventually, both black and white Cubans united to gain independence from Spain. The first revolt by white Cubans was in 1717. The Spanish reaction was swift and brutal. The army swiftly defeated the rebels, then hanged the survivors from trees by the roadside as a warning to others. The first time that black and white rebels in Cuba plotted together to force changes was in 1795. They wanted not only better trading conditions but also the abolition of slavery and the redistribution of land from the rich to the poor. The plot was discovered and the leaders punished, but the ideas did not die.

The last colonies

At the end of the eighteenth century, Cuba's fight for independence was encouraged by the success

After the Spanish had slaughtered most of the Indians, they brought slaves from other countries to Cuba. The slaves, both male and female, came mainly from Africa and China and were used to help grow and process sugarcane—the new source of Cuba's wealth.

of other countries' struggles, such as the American War of Independence and the slaves' revolt in Haiti. Soon, all of Spain's other Latin American colonies, such as Mexico, Venezuela, and Argentina had gained independence from Spain. By 1824, Cuba and Puerto Rico were Spain's only remaining colonies in the region. Cuba, Spain's "ever-faithful isle," was rewarded with improved trading conditions.

While some Cubans were pleased with the better prices they could now obtain, others still wanted independence and the abolition of slavery. Meanwhile, some of the richest slave-owning Cubans were frightened of the independence and antislavery feelings. They started to feel that they would be better protected by becoming part of North America. At the same time, North American politicians and traders began to feel that Cuba would be a valuable possession. They saw that Cuban products, especially sugar, could bring great profits if Cuba was opened to American business. In 1848, the American government offered $100 million to the Spanish government to buy Cuba. When the Spanish refused, some Americans decided to plan a series of invasions between 1848 and 1854. However, these plots were all discovered by the U.S. government in time to stop them.

The Ten Years' War

While the Americans' attention was diverted by the American Civil War (1861–1865), the Cubans continued to try to gain independence. On October 10, 1868, a group of 39 Cubans declared that they would fight for independence.

Their first leader was Carlos Manuel de Céspedes, who was a large landowner with many slaves. He freed his slaves, and they joined his rebel army. The rebel fighters, who called themselves *mambises*, were completely untrained and had few guns. Most had only their *machetes*, the heavy knives used for cutting sugarcane. The Spanish used all the soldiers they could muster to try to defeat the mambises, but although they had many more soldiers, they could not beat the Cubans. For ten years the fighting continued.

The Spanish army was trained to fight in ordered lines, but the Cubans had advantages in that they knew the landscape and had the support of most of the people. Instead of fighting big battles, the Cubans organized ambushes, then disappeared into the countryside. This style of fighting is known as guerrilla warfare, and it became a tradition for Cuban rebels to organize in this way.

The rebels had the support of whole communities. Cuban women played an important role in the fighting against the Spanish armies. As the women became involved, they saw the importance of their work, and felt that they should have equal rights with men. One of the leaders among the women, Ana Betancourt, became a leading campaigner for women's rights, and inspires many Cuban women to this day.

After ten years of fighting, 200,000 Spanish and 50,000 Cubans were dead, including Céspedes. Although the rebel army was still unbeaten, the leaders of the Cuban rebels accepted defeat. They signed a peace treaty in February 1878.

Antonio Maceo and José Martí

Antonio Maceo, one of the leaders who succeeded Céspedes, did not agree to the treaty and would not sign it. He believed that there should be no compromise with the Spanish, or with slave owners. When the treaty had been signed, he tried to organize a new rebellion, but was forced into exile. He went to Costa Rica.

Many other rebels also went into exile. Most of them went to the U.S. One, a 26-year-old teacher, first went to Spain, then on to the U.S. where he spent the next 15 years. His name was José Martí. While he was there, he watched events in Cuba carefully, and his friends in Cuba kept him informed of the ongoing struggle for freedom.

In 1892, Martí brought together many of the

The statue of the Cuban poet José Martí was put up in Havana to celebrate the part he played in helping the Cubans to achieve freedom. Martí helped to found the Cuban Revolutionary Party in 1892 and his writings inspire Cubans even today. He is known as the "father of the Cuban revolution."

people who wanted Cuban independence, and they formed the Cuban Revolutionary Party. In early 1895, they organized a new rebellion. Like the Ten Years' War, it started in the east of the island. Martí was killed in May, but Maceo, who had returned from Costa Rica, and Máximo Gómez, another leader, continued to lead the rebels. The Spanish once again brought all their mighty forces to Cuba, and once again faced the problem of trying to fight an army they could not catch. In desperation, they tried to destroy the rebels' support by imprisoning their sympathizers in prison camps. In order to cut off their supplies, they had to imprison whole villages. The prisoners suffered from terrible conditions in these camps and thousands died from disease and lack of food.

By 1898, it had become clear that the Spanish could not win the war. Maceo had been killed in December 1886, but the Cuban nationalists had nearly defeated the great Spanish army, which had become weak and demoralized. It seemed that at last independence would be won. However, at about the same time, the U.S. started to show greater interest in Cuban events.

3   The Twentieth Century

Until April 1898, the U.S. remained neutral in the Spanish-Cuban war. However, when an American ship, the *Maine*, was sunk in Havana harbor, the U.S. government decided to act. No one knew who had blown the ship up, but the U.S. government decided that America should declare war on the Spanish. By then, the Cubans had nearly defeated the Spanish. Two months later, the Spanish surrendered.

The Spanish surrender

When the Spanish army surrendered in Santiago de Cuba, it surrendered to the U.S. army, while the Cuban nationalists stood outside the city. The war has become known as the Spanish-American War, although the North Americans had lost only 266 soldiers while the Cubans had lost many thousands of soldiers and civilians. In the peace treaty, the U.S. took possession not only of Cuba, but also of Puerto Rico in the Caribbean, and the Philippines and Guam on the other side of the world in the Pacific Ocean.

The U.S. steps in

The U.S. army occupied Cuba until, in 1901, the Cuban leaders accepted an amendment to the constitution. It was called the Platt Amendment, after Senator Platt who proposed it to Congress. The amendment gave the U.S. the right to intervene in Cuban affairs at any time. It also stated that Cuba could not have an independent government. All the decision making had to be approved by the U.S. If it did not like what was going on in Cuba, the U.S. had the right to send in their army. When popular uprisings threatened the U.S.-backed government, the U.S. army was sent in. This occurred three times in the next 15 years. The U.S. was given a piece of land for a permanent naval base, in Guantanamo Bay. This naval base is still there today.

The next year, Cuba and the U.S. signed a trading agreement, by which the Cuban government agreed that import taxes would not be charged on American goods imported into Cuba. In return, the U.S. agreed to allow Cuban sugar and tobacco to enter the U.S. market without import taxes.

The effect of this agreement was to tie the economy of Cuba more closely with the economy

The Capitolio *is the seat of government in Havana. It was built as a replica of the Capitol building in Washington, D.C. However, behind the walls of Havana's Capitolio, for many years, there were politicians who had very little interest in the welfare of the people they represented.*

of the U.S. It meant that Cuba became dependent on the U.S. for nearly all its imports of goods. Within 15 years, 74 percent of all Cuba's imports came from the U.S. At the same time, Cuba became more and more dependent on the U.S. as the main customer for its exports. As more and more U.S. companies bought Cuban land and business, there was no major area of Cuban economic life that was not largely owned and controlled by U.S. interests.

Boom and slump

When World War I was being fought in Europe, the Cuban economy was booming because the sugar price was high. This is known in Cuban history books as the period of "the dance of the millions." Great fortunes were made by the American companies, who owned half the sugar harvest, and a few very rich Cuban plantation owners. Ordinary Cubans did not benefit.

Then, in 1920, the dance came to an end as the sugar price dropped from 22 cents a pound to only 3 cents a pound. Even worse times were ahead, when the Great Depression hit the U.S., and it slashed its imports from Cuba. The sugar workers, who had at least been able to eat during the "dance of the millions," found that their wages were cut and there was less work. During the quiet season between sugar harvests, there was no work at all and very little to eat. Sometimes, survival meant eating roots and locusts, and living in the woods and in caves.

The sugar price and trading links with the U.S. continued to affect the lives of Cubans for many years. As economic links with the U.S. grew,

Sugarcane provided most of Cuba's wealth for many years. It gave work, though low-paying, to many Cubans, cutting, stacking, and processing the cane. In 1920, the price of sugar plunged and many of the workers lost their jobs. There was very little other work.

more Americans visited Cuba, and Cubans ate more American food, heard more American music, and wore more American clothes.

America's playground

As time went by, Cuba was discovered by rich Americans as a place to build their dream homes. Vast luxury mansions were built on the most beautiful beaches. As rich Americans arrived to spend their holidays, a tourist industry grew. Apart from beaches, the tourists came to spend their money at the bars, spectacular cabarets, and gambling casinos which flourished in Havana, alongside the luxury hotels and restaurants.

From the Cubans' point of view, the visitors brought money and work, in all the jobs

31

providing services to the rich visitors. Life for ordinary workers, especially those struggling to make a living in the countryside, was harsh. Often there was not enough food, and families faced starvation. They came to the towns, especially to Havana, to do any work they could find, often for very low wages and in terrible conditions, just to feed themselves and their families. Children, as well as adults, had to work to make enough to live.

Corruption in high places

The political system in these years was officially democratic. There were regular elections, and according to the constitution there was freedom of expression. However, the reality was often very different. With so much wealth in so few hands, rich people controlled those in positions of power. Elections were often marked by corruption; candidates won votes by paying or threatening voters. Successful politicians used public funds for themselves while some police officers cooperated with gangsters.

People protested against corruption and inefficiency, and asked for measures to improve their standard of living, but the lives of the poor remained hard. Sometimes the Cubans' protests won victories. In 1920, students seized the University of Havana in protest of the corruption and incompetence at the university, and some changes were made. In 1933, a revolution forced the president to flee from Cuba. As people were not satisfied by the next president, he was forced to resign by an army rebellion supported by workers and students.

Life for many Cubans was very hard and they lived in great poverty. There were often only shacks for homes, not enough food or clothing, and there was virtually no health care or education. In rural areas the people often starved.

People who opposed the government had to be brave. The army and the police were used by governments to arrest, torture, and kill opponents. In one rebellion in 1912, 3,000 people were killed. On other occasions, demonstrators were fired upon and leaders of opposition groups were assassinated.

The Cuban People's Party

In 1933, General Fulgencio Batista had used the army to take control of Cuba. When his hand-picked candidate was defeated in 1944, Cubans hoped for a return to a democracy and improvements in the lives of ordinary Cubans. Instead, they found that the new leaders were as corrupt as any before, and brutal in their treatment of opponents. In 1952, a general election was due to be held. A new, popular political party, the Cuban People's Party, known as the *Ortodoxo*, had promised to run an honest government and to end corrupt practices.

As the elections of 1952 drew near, the opinion polls broadcast the popularity of the Ortodoxo party. General Batista was also running for election. The polls showed that he was only the third most popular candidate. He decided that he would not wait for the election, and organized a successful military coup. Cuba was ruled once again by the army.

A young lawyer, who was a supporter of the Ortodoxo, tried to take Batista to court, to have him thrown into jail for taking power illegally. The lawyer's name was Fidel Castro. When he lost his case, he resolved to work in whatever way he could to rid Cuba of Batista's military rule.

The revolution begins

Since Batista had taken power through a coup, there was no democratic system in place to oppose Batista legally. Therefore, Fidel Castro and others started to plot secretly. Their first plan was to take over a large barracks in the south of the island, at Moncada, and to get the soldiers to join them. The plan failed. Half of the small band of conspirators were killed and Fidel Castro was arrested. He was sentenced with the other prisoners to 15 years in prison on the Isle of Pines.

Meanwhile, a popular campaign for their release began in Cuba. On May 13, 1955, Batista agreed to free all the Moncada prisoners. They returned in triumph to Havana, with Fidel Castro greeted as their leader. They quickly set about organizing an opposition movement called the "26 July Movement." July 26, 1953, was the date of the attack on Moncada. Soon it became clear that Batista's government could not accept such a popular opposition movement. Fidel Castro was prevented from making public speeches, while other members of the group were re-arrested or threatened. The government terrorized the people to suppress all opposition. In vain, the Ortodoxos, trade unionists, communists, and other groups including groups of professionals all tried to protest against Batista's military rule. Batista could rely on U.S. support. U.S. advisers were sent to Cuba to help set up a "Bureau to Repress Communist Activities."

Fidel Castro was forced into exile because of the repression. He went to the U.S. and continued his work from there. He traveled up and down the East Coast, where thousands of Cuban emigrants and exiles were living, collecting money for his movement. Then he found a Cuban who was able to help him to train young revolutionaries on a ranch in Mexico.

Castro's army
Finally, in November 1956, Castro's little army was ready. They set sail in a small pleasure yacht, called the *Granma*, bound for the east of Cuba with 82 revolutionaries on board. After a rough journey they faced Batista's forces. The first battle was disastrous. Most of Castro's men died or were captured. The tiny group of young adventurers that was left certainly could not

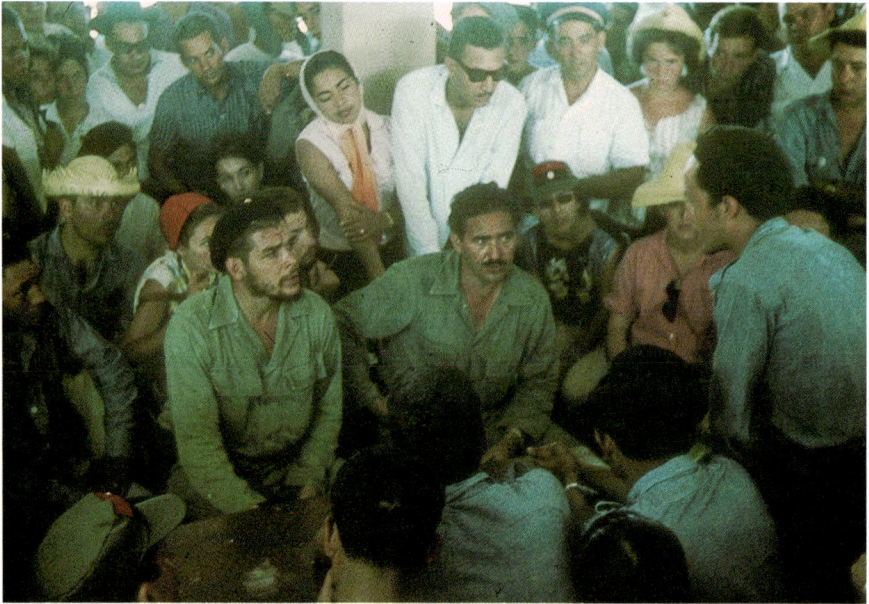

The Argentinian revolutionary, Ché Guevara, joined Fidel Castro in 1956 to help with the revolutionary war. He wanted to make governments change so that they cared for the poor. Ché Guevara instructed young Cubans in the art of guerrilla warfare and became one of Castro's chief lieutenants in the war.

defeat Batista's army, but they had two important things in their favor. First, the people of the mountains were strong opponents of Batista, and so they found a warm welcome. Second, Batista's army and equipment was unsuited to the fighting conditions in mountainous tropical forests. So Fidel's small, determined army was gradually able to conquer the whole of the Sierra Maestra mountain range.

The people rally

As they fought, more and more people came to join the rebels while others in towns organized the supply of food and weapons. The rebels' radio station told the rest of the population about their cause. The time had come for all people to take sides. Anyone who helped the rebels faced terrible dangers, from the army, police, and from private armies. Eventually, people started to organize themselves and the streets became like battlegrounds. Support for the rebellion increased and, by May 1958, the rebel army was ready to move.

Batista had 10,000 men gathered around the foothills of the mountains, but they could not win. In a famous battle, in which the rebels surrounded the government forces, Castro found out that the leader of the enemy troops, José Quevedo, had been a fellow university student. He invited him to change sides. At first, Quevedo refused, but eventually, he and his soldiers were won over to the rebels' cause. The guerrilla army left the mountains, and advanced across the plains, northwest toward Havana.

Victory
The last great battle was at Santa Clara. When Batista heard the news of the rebels' victory, he packed his bags and left, like other dictators before him. The army tried to set up a government, but the people had had enough of them. There was a general strike. There was also complete confusion in the streets. Crowds of people entered the gambling casinos, smashing the machines. They burned the offices of the newspaper that had supported Batista, and smashed parking meters, which had been used to collect money for the hated government. They also opened the prisons to free all the political prisoners.

Fidel Castro, the guerrilla fighter Ché Guevara,

and their army entered Havana triumphantly on January 9, 1959. A million people were on the streets to greet them, and hear them announce that this revolution was going to bring about a more equal and just society.

The new revolutionary government
When a new government was formed, the young rebel leaders were not part of it at first, but soon the prime minister resigned and Castro replaced him in response to popular demand. Taking power from Batista had been difficult, but the difficulties were by no means over once the rebels were able to form their own government. They were determined to get down to the roots of the corruption and poverty in Cuban society and take steps to eliminate them.

During Batista's seven years of military rule, 20,000 Cubans had been killed and many more had been tortured. The families of his victims now wanted justice, and that meant the death penalty for the worst criminals. After public trials, when the gruesome evidence of mass graves and photographs of victims were shown, executions were carried out swiftly. Many who had done well under Batista's rule thought that they might be the next victims, and fled.

The Agricultural Reform Law
The people who owned large amounts of property knew that they were not popular with the new government. The revolutionaries believed that it was unjust that wealthy owners of huge farms paid their workers less than a living wage. Landowners in the towns and in the

countryside charged their tenants rents so high that they had little left to live on. As the landowners feared, the new government took the bold step of taking the land from the rich. An Agricultural Reform Law in May 1959 transferred the ownership of 40 percent of all land, with huge farms being taken by the state, and small tenant farms given to those who had rented them.

For tenants in the cities, the government reduced the amount of rent that the landlords could charge by 50 percent. With the same

The landowning and professional Cubans lived very well. They were often extremely wealthy. Havana has many stately houses that, before the revolution, were owned by such people and are now used as public buildings or converted into apartments.

boldness, telephone charges were also cut by 50 percent. More changes were promised, to raise wages, bring down electricity prices, and provide education and health care for all. These measures were very popular with the poor, but not with the landowners or the utility companies.

Cuba and the U.S. become enemies
The electricity and telephone companies and many of the large farms and city properties were owned by companies and people in the U.S. These companies' managers and the landowners felt that what the Cuban government was doing was not only illegal but also dangerous, as it threatened the principle of property ownership. Gradually, the U.S. government turned against the new Cuban government. In June 1959, to show its disapproval, the U.S. cut the amount of sugar that it would buy from Cuba. When the Cubans showed no sign of changing their policies, all sugar imports to the U.S. from Cuba were canceled. If sugar could not be sold to earn money to buy essential imports, the Cuban economy could collapse. However, the plan backfired when the Soviet Union offered to buy the sugar instead.

Nationalization
The next shock to American business was the announcement that Cuba was not going to buy oil from the U.S. since it could find cheaper oil elsewhere. Castro ordered the American-owned oil refineries to refine oil that Cuba was getting from Venezuela. When the oil companies refused to do this the Cuban government started to

nationalize the oil refineries. Eventually, the U.S. struck back by halting all trade with Cuba. In turn, Castro took over all remaining American business. In January 1961, the American government finally broke off diplomatic relations with Cuba. It believed that taking property that was legally owned by American businesses was illegal. Meanwhile, the Cuban government had set up a ministry which took property away from those who had won it by working with the illegal Batista government.

Relations with the U.S. got even worse after an attempt by U.S. armed exiles to invade Cuba from the Bay of Pigs in April 1961. The invasion was defeated swiftly by the Cubans. The whole episode was a shock to the U.S. policy makers and made them realize that the Cuban revolution had more support than they thought.

The exiles with U.S. support had tried invasion, but failed. The U.S. had also tried to increase the economic pressure, by halting all trade with Cuba. This presented great problems for the Cubans, but they would not change their policies. The final crisis came in October 1962.

The Cuban Missile Crisis

When the U.S. navy started to gather its forces in the seas around Cuba, for military exercises, Cubans felt that they were under threat of direct invasion. Ché Guevara went to Moscow to ask for help. The Soviet Union installed missiles to insure Cuba's defense. The U.S. felt that Cuban missile sites would be capable of launching Soviet-backed attacks against U.S. cities and were a threat to world peace. The U.S. president,

John F. Kennedy, said that if the missiles were not withdrawn, war would be declared on Cuba.

The whole world watched with horror at this unfolding of the real threat of nuclear war between the U.S. and the Soviet Union. In the end, the "Cuban Missile Crisis" passed peacefully. The U.S. promised that there would be no more attempts to invade Cuba, and the Soviet Union withdrew the missiles. Nonetheless, Cuba and the U.S. continue to be hostile to each other to this day. The involvement of the Soviet Union in Cuban affairs had increased the tension between the U.S. and Cuba. As Cuba was becoming a close ally of the Soviet Union, its relations with the U.S. deteriorated. In April 1961, Castro announced that the revolution was "socialist," and in December 1961, he announced that it was a communist revolution, opposed to the capitalist system of the U.S.

The transformation of Cuba

Since 1959, Cuba has changed so much that it is impossible to discuss any aspect of life in Cuba without discussing the changes "since the revolution." Fidel Castro and the guerrillas wanted to free Cuba of gangsterism and corruption, and to improve the lives of the poor. In the countryside, they had seen the problems of unemployment, poverty, and hunger. They pledged that they would introduce reforms so that small farmers could own their own land instead of paying high rents to rich landowners, and to give the sugar workers better working conditions and work throughout the year. To rid

Cuba of hunger and disease, food would need to become available for everyone. Food rationing and the right to free health care and education have become part of life since 1959. These were big ambitions for a small country which depended mainly on a single crop—sugar—and where there were not enough people who had a good education. The difficulties were complicated by the hostilities of the U.S. which created a feeling that Cuba was being threatened. The economic blockade, followed by military aggression, assassination attempts, and industrial sabotage made it very difficult for Cuba to achieve economic growth and stability.

On the other hand, this threat brought people together to work hard to make the reforms successful, as it brought the need for strong political unity. People who disagreed with Castro were thought to be acting on the side of the U.S. All newspapers were controlled by the government and it was decided that there should be only one political party, the Communist party, to bring stability to the country.

Although there now is only one political party in Cuba, there are many other organizations, such as the Federation of Cuban Women, the school childrens' and students' groups, trade unions, and farmers' associations. These groups suggest changes and discuss the policies of the Communist party and of the elected National Assembly. When there is an important national decision to be made, there is a referendum, and each adult Cuban can vote for or against it. This is how the system of elected assemblies was introduced, by a referendum in 1976.

Dr. Fidel Castro Ruz has been president of Cuba since the revolution in 1959. For many years there were no elections, but in 1976 elections were held and Dr. Castro was formally elected president. In 1989 he celebrated 30 years as Cuba's ruler.

However, questions usually require discussion and cannot be decided by a simple yes or no answer to a simple question. That is why Cubans are encouraged to discuss national and local problems in schools, factories, and farms throughout the country. After years of elections which were supposed to be democratic but which always brought more corrupt rulers, most people think that the system they have is more democratic than the one it replaced in 1959. The lack of freedom to organize any opposition to the Communist government is seen as the price to be paid for such improvements to the health and living standards of most of the Cuban people.

4

A Healthy, Well-educated Population

Some of the most dramatic changes in Cuba since Fidel Castro's government took over in 1959 have been in health and education. Since then, a large proportion of the national income has been put into both these services.

The Cuban government has set up an excellent and much-needed free health service. Up-to-date hospitals have the latest equipment. The Hermanos Almejeiras hospital in Havana has an international reputation for success in complicated surgery.

The Cuban health service is now one of the best in the world. Its development in the past 30 years is remarkable. In the 1950s, the average life expectancy was over 60. Today, Cubans can expect to live to 75, just as they would in a rich country. The average figures for life expectancy in the 1950s were comparable to other Latin American nations; but for the poor, life

45

expectancy was very low. The worst suffering
was among the poor people who lived in the
countryside. Even if they could manage to travel
the long distances in time to find a doctor, they
might not get any treatment unless they could
find enough money to pay the medical fees.

Children used to die of many diseases, such as
typhoid, diptheria, tetanus, and gastroenteritis,
which can all be prevented by better health
standards. Lack of adequate food and simple
hygiene facilities weakened children's resistance
to disease.

In 1958, there were only 6,000 doctors in the
whole country, and most of those were in
Havana. There was only one medical school in
Cuba and admission was very competitive. When
the new government came to power in 1959,
about half of the doctors left Cuba and went to the
U.S. The hospitals did not have enough available
beds for the patients, and there were not enough
doctors.

New hospitals, more doctors
The urgent task of building new hospitals and
training new doctors was started. Some new
hospitals were built, while other hospitals used
buildings that had been large houses or hotels. In
order to bring health care quickly to the
countryside, the Medical Rural Service was
created in January 1960. After becoming
qualified, every doctor would have to spend two
years working in the rural areas.

There are now nearly 300 hospitals, equipped
with the latest technology. The advanced
technology now used in Cuban hospitals has

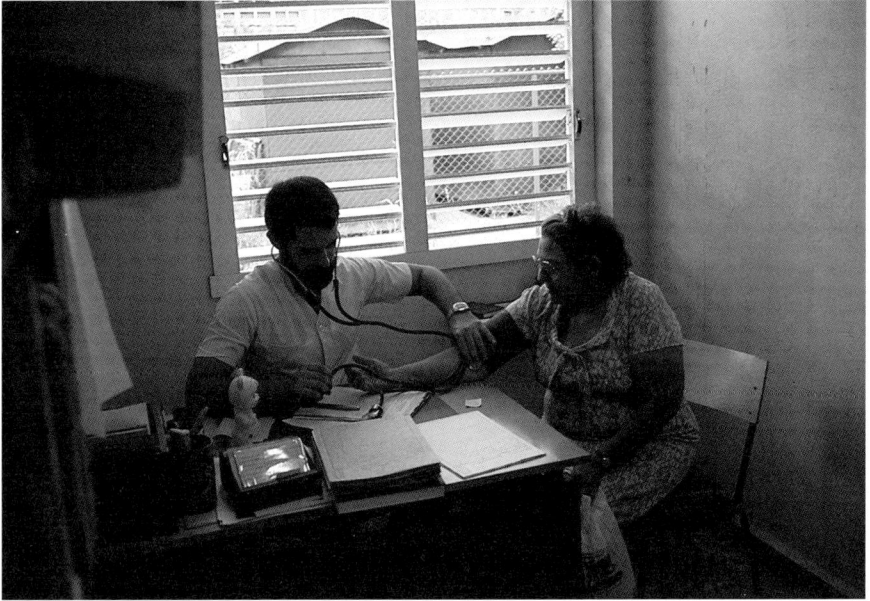

There are nearly 23,000 doctors in Cuba, many of whom are in general practice. They often have their clinics in their own homes but some travel out to remoter areas.

brought important successes in the fields of heart transplants and plastic surgery. There is now one doctor in Cuba for every 450 people, and one dentist for every 1,864 people. There is one medical school in each province and there are 27,000 medical science students, including nurses and paramedical technicians.

Prevention is better than cure
Today, to continue to improve the health of the Cuban people it is necessary to make them aware of the importance of a balanced diet and the dangers of smoking cigarettes. For this reason, a major health education program has become a central part of the health care service. A lot of education is needed to help Cubans give up their

habits of consuming Cuba's main crops, sugar and tobacco. When food rations or vouchers were first introduced to ensure that everyone had enough food to stay healthy, cigarettes were included. Now, cigarettes are no longer included in the ration, except for those who are already addicted and feel too old to change.

Cubans generally enjoy being plump because it is a sign of health compared with the malnutrition of the recent past. However, extra weight is now recognized as a health problem that can lead to heart disease, and people are encouraged to eat less fat and exercise more. Sports facilities are available for everyone and Cuba has produced many world-class sports figures.

In 1982, a new "family doctor" service was introduced in some country areas. Doctors were

Cubans are happy to donate blood to their hospitals, and there are special clinics where the blood is taken. These clinics provide a sterile atmosphere and the donor can remain anonymous.

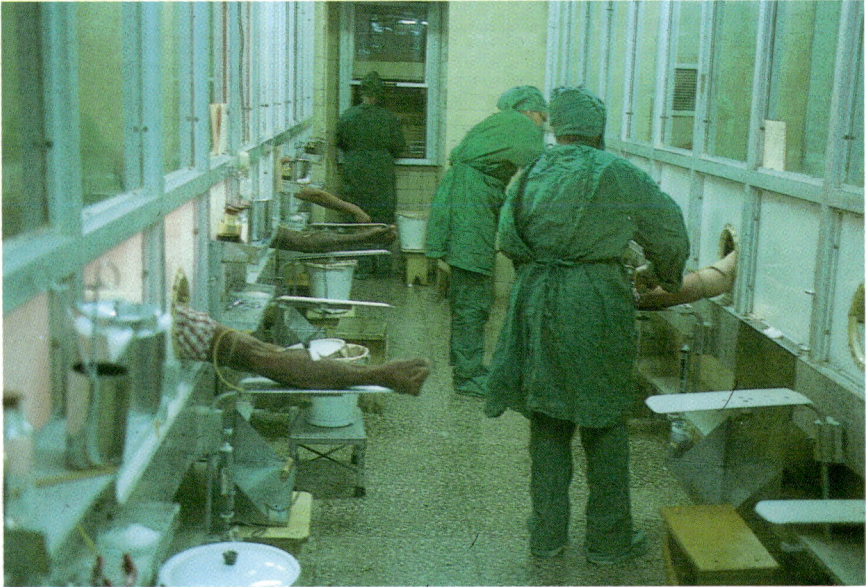

each given a small area, in which they were able to visit all their patients, on horseback if necessary. This meant that patients did not have to travel to their nearest local hospital, or "polyclinic" and doctors got to know their patients well. This service was very successful and now it has been extended; plans are that by the year 2000 it will cover the whole country.

Looking after children
The death rate among newborn babies has been reduced dramatically. In 1959, one child in every 20 could be expected to die in the first year of its life. Since 1979, the infant death rate has fallen to about the same level as the much richer countries of North America and western Europe. Cuba has achieved this by devoting great energy to the care of infants. There are new facilities for detecting diseases or potential problems in pregnant women and newborn infants. A laboratory has been set up in each province, for the purpose of checking mothers and babies, so that no one is missed. A special budget is set aside especially for children's hospitals, which are well equipped with the most advanced technology.

Such a good health service is not cheap, but for Cubans it is a symbol of the new society they are trying to build. While there are difficulties and shortages in other areas of their lives, they know that when they or their children are sick, there will be someone to care for them.

Education for all
The Cuban people seem to love learning. One-third of the whole Cuban population attends

some kind of classes regularly. That includes tiny children at day-care centers as well as grandparents attending night schools. Today, there are hardly any people who cannot at least read and write, even though Cuba is still not a rich country. In 1959, the picture was very different, as many people could not read or write. Although the law stated that primary education was to be available to all people, many children did not get any education at all. For example, children who lived in the countryside had to help their parents on the farms. It was estimated that there were about one million illiterate people. In 1960, a new plan was introduced to teach illiterate working adults. It was so successful that by the end of 1961, illiteracy in Cuba had been reduced to about three percent of the population.

Day-care centers
From the very early age of only three or four months, many children go to day-care centers, which are open from 7:00 a.m. to 7:00 p.m. The Cubans decided that without day-care centers there would never be real equality of men and women at work. There are still not enough places for all those that want them, but the government continues to provide more. The main organization which argued for day-care centers was the Federation of Cuban Women. This powerful organization campaigns for equality of opportunity between men and women. It has also written a "family code," which sets out the equal rights and duties for men and women in the family in the new Cuba. Although many men are taking a long time to learn to do their share of

As the number of jobs increases, more women wish to work, so day-care centers for small children are provided. These are well equipped and the children are well cared for and given activities to develop various skills.

household duties, the family code has been read and discussed by everyone, and there is a feeling that the old-fashioned division of labor at home will steadily be removed.

The battle for the sixth grade
In the 1970s there was a national campaign to make sure that all Cubans had a basic education.

This campaign was called "the battle for the sixth grade." The sixth grade is the level of education reached by children when they are at the age of about 11. It includes learning to read and write, to do arithmetic, and to have a minimum level of general knowledge. When they are five, all Cuban children must go to primary school. All schooling is free, with free transportation, school uniforms, equipment, materials, books, and food. Children also learn to play musical instruments and to sing, dance, and paint.

To make sure that everybody had achieved the sixth grade, the adults who had missed out on school had to be educated, too. Since they could not stop working to go to school, they had to learn at evening classes and classes held at factories,

The large, open campus of this secondary school was built during the 1970s, as were most other secondary schools. Before this time there were not enough educated Cubans who could benefit from secondary education. The school has good sports facilities, including a swimming pool.

Cuban university students study hard for their examinations. Both boys and girls are encouraged to go to college where the education is free.

farms, and offices all over the country. To provide the books needed for this learning, libraries were set up in all towns, and mobile libraries were sent to the remotest country districts. The battle for the sixth grade was won in 1980. The Cubans have now set themselves a new target, the battle for the ninth grade. The adult education programs continue, and learning has become one of the most popular pastimes for Cubans.

Secondary and higher educaton

After completing the sixth grade, at about 11 years of age, children go to secondary school. There are no single-sex schools in Cuba. Most of the secondary schools were built after 1970, when enough people had achieved the sixth grade and were looking forward to taking their education further.

José Martí believed that children should learn about practical things as well as things that could be learned from books. These ideas have led to the building of "schools in the countryside," which are weekly boarding schools for secondary pupils. At these schools, the students spend half of their day working in the fields and the other half studying. The agricultural work helps them to learn to work together and to understand how food is produced, as well as helping to pay for the education system. The schools also bring together children from different backgrounds, bringing country children and town children together. Children with special learning needs are provided with special education. For those who have needs which cannot be met within ordinary schools, there are over 400 special schools with a total of about 40,000 students.

Secondary schooling finishes at ninth grade, which is when the pupils are 14 years old. They then leave their secondary schools to go to a specialized school until the age of 17. There are technical schools, teachers' training schools, and pre-university schools to choose from. In order to go to these schools students must pass exams.

Universities, like all other levels of education, are free, and students receive a small income so that they are no longer dependent on their families. Cuba has four universities and nearly 30 other higher education institutes, scattered around the country. In all, nearly a quarter of a million students are continuing their studies into higher education.

International health and education

Every year, thousands of Cuban doctors and teachers work abroad, in many countries in Latin America, Africa, and Asia. Cuban students also go to study abroad, mainly to other communist countries, such as the Soviet Union. They can then bring back home skills in new technologies to help Cuba to become more self-reliant. Meanwhile, thousands of overseas students study in Cuba, such as students from a number of African countries.

5

People and Culture

The Cuban people today are descended mostly from the Spanish and Africans who arrived in Cuba over the past 500 years. If you look at a group of Cubans you will find a mixture of black, white, and brown skins. There are also traces of Chinese, as about 200,000 Chinese people were brought in to Cuba in the nineteenth century to work in the sugar industry. Originally, they came as "contracted labor," on an eight year contract. However, at the end of the eight years, they could not afford to return home, so they stayed on and became Cubans.

At first, the different racial groups lived separately. Then, over the years, they gradually

The huge Colón cemetery in Havana is filled with elaborate gravestones and family mausoleums. The Cubans see honoring their dead as an important part of life. The islanders mainly follow the Roman Catholic religion although there is no official state religion.

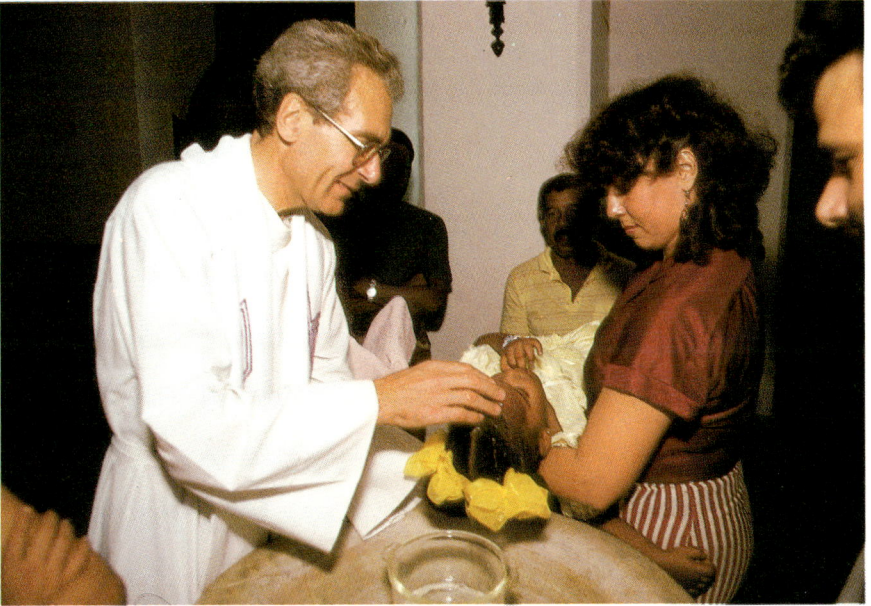

Most children are baptized when they are quite small, usually babies. It is seen as an important family event. However, the children do not necessarily attend church regularly when they grow up.

started to live together in the same neighborhoods. All these different immigrants brought with them their traditions and way of life, and now Cuban traditions, festivals, music, dance, and religions all show aspects of the different groups.

Spanish Catholicism

Spanish conquerors brought the Roman Catholic religion to Cuba. As soon as they arrived, the Spanish started to build churches, and there are still some surviving today that date back to the time of the earliest Spanish arrivals.

In the first few years after the 1959 revolution, relations between the church and the revolutionary government were not good. The new government was determined to break up the power of the church. The government arrested many of the people who protested and sent them to prison.

Today, there is an uneasy peace between the government and the church. There are no religious schools, but Catholics and people of other religions are permitted to worship as they wish. The government gives money to the churches, to help them to maintain their church buildings, and supports their charity work. It is estimated that about half of all Cubans today believe in the Catholic religion, but the number of believers has been falling for many years, even before the revolution. Only about one person in twenty actually goes to church regularly.

Other religions

Apart from the Catholics, there are also a smaller number of Protestants. Some of these arrived in Cuba over many years from the English-speaking Caribbean islands, such as Jamaica. They also have churches which have regular services. There are over 1,000 pastors of the various Protestant churches, although nearly 75 percent of the pastors who were in Cuba in 1959 have left.

There is also a small Jewish community in Havana. Most of the Jews who came to Cuba came at the beginning of the twentieth century from Turkey and the eastern Mediterranean, and others came just before or during World War II. Now there are only about 1,500 Jews in Cuba, and there is only one synagogue that holds services in the whole of the country. There are also some social centers run for the Jewish community, and these get help from the government. As there is no *kosher* food produced in Cuba, Jews receive parcels sent from the Canadian Jewish community with the special food they need.

Religions from Africa

The Africans in Cuba did not forget their religion and culture when they arrived in Cuba. The slave owners tried to stop them from worshiping their own gods, and tried to convert them to Catholicism. Some slaves started to worship in secret, while others adapted their forms of worship so that they would not be punished.

In secret societies, the slaves' beliefs and customs were handed down from parents to children, so they survived over the centuries. The survival of these religions is remarkable. Recently, Cubans have gone to Africa to learn about the culture and religions from which the slaves were taken. They were looking for similarities between the Afro-Cuban religions and those that exist now in Africa. They were very surprised to find that many of the beliefs and ceremonies were almost exactly the same as those in Africa.

Some of the slaves found that the best way to keep their religion was not to worship in secret, but to appear to accept the Catholic faith. They worshiped Catholic saints, but in fact they were only giving the names of Catholic saints to their own spirits. The most widespread of these adapted religions, which is called Santeria, was created by the people of the Yoruba society of west Africa.

While the Spanish Catholics were having

religious festivals on the saints' days, the Yorubas would join in these festivals. They would seem to be worshiping the Spanish Catholic saints, but in fact were worshiping the spirits of their dead ancestors to which they had given the saints' names. They would perform the dances and songs of their own Yoruba traditions. Some of these dances can still be seen at carnival time. At the end of July, the whole of Cuba goes carnival crazy. Local street organizations get together for weeks before to prepare the carnival floats and costumes. Each major town has its own carnival, which draws on the traditions of the people who live there.

In Santiago de Cuba an enthusiastic audience attends a troubador house to hear traditional Cuban music. The trobadores *are all men. They accompany their singing with the drum and guitar, both of which are traditional instruments.*

Music and dance

Most Cubans love music. From infancy to old age, they dance. The instruments they use and the rhythms they play reflect their history. The guitar

60

from Spain, drums from Africa, and trumpets playing American jazz music combine to give a rich and varied range of sounds.

The Spanish brought their ballad-singing tradition with classical Spanish guitar music. They sang stories from their lives, as well as Catholic religious themes. This style of singing still survives in the music of the *trobadores* which developed in the countryside. In each town there is now a troubador house where people can meet and express their feelings in music. One famous singer in this tradition is Carlos Puebla, who wrote songs about the revolution. In the traditional Spanish *serenade*, in Cuba, most of the singing is done by the men. The old men sing of their hard lives and the young sing of love.

Cubans enjoy all forms of dance, whether it is at a carnival, traditional folk dance, or the more formal modern dance. This dance troupe is performing a new dance developed to celebrate the struggles of the revolution.

Carnivals

The small *bongos*, the medium-sized *tumbadores*, and the large *tambores* are three different types of African drum. African music could first be heard in Cuba in the *barracas*, the slaves' quarters on the sugar plantations. The Spanish slave owners at first tried to forbid this singing. The slaves found that the only time when they were allowed to sing and dance was on the days that the Spanish had religious festivities. They adopted some elements of the Spanish melodies, but added the African rhythms and percussions, to make their own version of the festivities.

Apart from the festival and carnival times, African music was played in secret. Anyone found playing the music would be punished. It was not until the end of the nineteenth century that the music started to appear in public. One of the first ways in which the music was heard was in the songs of street traders.

Modern music

Young Cubans now dance to a sound which is similar to the *salsa* heard in other parts of Latin America, but the Cuban version is called the *son*. There are a bewildering number of dances performed during the street parties and house parties, and the music changes constantly with each new musician's imagination.

There are also musicians influenced by the trobadores who added some modern rock to make what Cubans call *Nueva Trova* style. This movement started in Cuba in the late 1960s. It was influenced by the developments in rock music and folk music at that time in other parts of the world, but drew on the Cuban experience. Another Cuban contribution to modern music is the distinct style of Cuban jazz. The most internationally famous group, Iraker, includes individual musicians who are recognized among the world's best.

Cubans learn to dance as soon as they can stand, so it is not surprising that the standards for professional dancers are very high. Besides a national classical ballet, Cuba also has an internationally famous modern ballet, and also a folk ballet. The *Folklórico* performs dances taken from African dances, which are being carefully researched by students of dance. People from all over the world go to Havana's school of folkloric dance, to learn about the Afro-Cuban heritage.

The drum meets the guitar
The Africans brought their musical rhythms and dance to Cuba. By the 1940s, there were four distinct types of Afro-Cuban music: the Colombia, which is a dance for men only, showing strength; the rumba, the fastest music, with dances for men and women; the yambus, a quieter, softer music; and the guaguanco, with songs about life, love, and injustice. If there were no drums handy, the musicians would use spoons, forks, and boxes to keep the rhythm.

In Cuba today, all these elements of traditional Cuban music are kept alive. People still play guitars in town squares and pick up drums to start a dance at parties. On the radio, the bands which specialize in the various styles can be heard all day long, their music drifting out of the houses into the streets.

Literature

While Cuba was a Spanish colony, educated people looked to Europe for their literature. As a result, there was very little Cuban literature based on the culture and society of the island itself. One exception was the work of Cirilo Villaverde, in the nineteenth century. He wrote about life in Cuba, and the feelings of people caught up in a society divided between rich and poor, Spanish and Cuban, black and white. His most famous novel, *Cecilia*, is a tale of a woman who is courted by two men—the son of a slave trader, and an organizer of a slave rebellion. For Cubans today, it gives a clear picture of the attitudes and lifestyles of their country's past. Now that all Cubans are able to read, there is a great demand for all kinds of books. To encourage reading, the government ensures that books are very inexpensive. The only difficulty is in producing enough of them. It is often difficult to find a particular book, because the shops are always out of stock. Although more books are now written by Cuban authors than ever before, there is still a great demand for foreign literature.

Movies and television

Until 1959, almost all the movies seen in Cuba were made in the U.S., and so Cuba has made a great effort to build its own film industry. Cuba is building links with the growing Latin American film industry, to create a Latin American film tradition. A new Latin American film school has been opened in Havana, and an annual Havana film festival shows an international audience the year's best movies from Cuba, Latin America, and other parts of the world.

Cuban television is in some ways very different from television in most parts of the world. For example, there are no commercial breaks. When President Fidel Castro makes an important speech, it is often screened in full, which sometimes means hours of continuous talking. On the other hand, there are soap operas, thrillers, music programs, and lots of cartoons. There is even a regular slot for new films from the U.S. Although there is still a political barrier between Cuba and the U.S., Cubans have not lost their interest in the culture of their northern neighbor. Now, they also see many programs from other parts of the world, especially Latin America, the Soviet Union, and Spain.

6

Life in the Countryside

Cuba's countryside ranges from low-lying swamp lands to rugged mountain ranges, with wide plains and rolling hills in between. With lush vegetation and brightly colored flowers, the countryside is very beautiful, especially in the mountain areas, where wild plants grow freely.

Farm workers, or campesions, live in small *houses called* bohios. *This bohio is thatched with palm leaves or grasses and the walls are built of palm wood, which are the traditional materials used for centuries. Now some bohios are built from factory-made materials and the porch around this bohio is roofed with corrugated iron.*

King sugar

The most important crop grown in Cuba is sugar. Sugar production covers half of all the land under cultivation and sugar workers and their families account for 16 percent of the entire population of the island nation.

In the sugar industry, most of the farms are big plantations which are now owned by the government. One of the first acts of the new government in 1959 was to pass a land reform law. This took land away from the owners of the huge sugar plantations. It also took land away from other landowners who rented their land to tenant farmers. The big sugar plantations were made into state farms.

Slaves used to harvest the sugar with machetes, which was extremely hard work. When slavery was abolished, the working conditions of sugar workers were still very harsh. They were paid barely enough to live on, and were without work when there was no sugar to be harvested. However, farm owners found it cheaper to employ plenty of low-wage workers than to buy machinery.

Now, some of the sugar is still cut by hand with machetes, but the hours are shorter and the wages much higher. The workers are employed by the state Ministry of Sugar and paid a salary. In fact, sugar cutters are now among the highest-paid manual workers in the country. Some of the work is done by volunteers who normally do other jobs. These volunteers are carefully selected now. In the past, many of the eager volunteers turned out to be worse than useless, since they were too weak to handle the machetes.

It has been a high priority for the government to introduce sugar-cutting machines into the industry. These sugar-cutting machines can do the work of many people, but they are very expensive. About 60 percent of the harvesting is now done by machines.

This enormous sugarcane mill dominates the surrounding countryside. It is located about 100 miles (160 kilometers) from Havana and is one of the 164 mills that process sugarcane. Cuba produces nearly seven million tons of sugarcane, which makes it the second largest sugar producer in the world.

Processing sugarcane

When the cane has been cut, it has to be taken quickly to the sugar mills for it will quickly decay if left outside for too long in the heat. Special railways on the big plantations hurry the sugar to the mill. When the cane arrives at the mill it has to be crushed, boiled, purified, evaporated, and then spun before sugar is made from it. Sugarcane does not only make sugar, though. In the production process, a black syrup called molasses is produced. It is a food which can be used in cooking or to feed animals. The fiber that comes from the cane, called bagasse, is used for fuel as well as being useful in the production of paper, cardboard, and even as a wood substitute for furniture and building. Even the leaves of the sugarcane are used, as an ingredient in the production of plastics.

About ten percent of all the sugar harvested goes to the rum factories. There are eight of these factories, and the processes used in them are based on traditions that go back hundreds of years. The longer the rum stays in its barrel, the darker it gets, so the best rums are a rich brown.

Cuba's famous tobacco

Tobacco farmers, unlike sugar workers, usually own their own small piece of land. The valleys of the northwest region of Cuba, Pinar del Rio, are famous for producing the very best-quality tobacco. Tobacco grows well in Cuba because the soil is fertile and the climate hot and damp. Tobacco is treated with great care and respect by all the people who grow it and process it. Harvest

Shriveled brown tobacco leaves hang in a drying shed until they are right for making into the famous Havana cigars. The walls of the drying hut are loosely thatched with palm leaves to let the air circulate easily.

time is between November and February. The farmers have to know exactly when the plant is ready to be cut, which must be judged carefully by watching the size and color of the leaves.

When it has been cut, the tobacco leaf has to be dried. After about four days drying in the sun, the leaves are taken into drying houses, where they will hang for about another 40 days. The large drying houses can be recognized easily, situated always with the doors at each end facing east and west. This is to ensure that the leaves are never scorched by the direct rays of the sun, so that they can dry slowly to keep their full natural flavor.

The leaves are sorted according to smell and color. Then they are taken to the cigar and cigarette factories. While the cigarettes are made in automated factories, the production of cigars cannot be hurried. Cuban cigars require so much labor that they are expensive, but the price reflects a quality that cannot be matched by mechanized production. Work in the cigar factories is highly skilled, and takes a long time to learn well. Some of the presses where cigars are placed to give them a good shape are over 100 years old.

Cigar factory workers have traditionally been better paid than other workers because of their skills. They have also been better educated, because of the tradition, started nearly 200 years ago and continued to this day, of having one of the workers sitting at a high desk at the front of the factory hall, reading to the other workers. Poetry and novels from all over the world, as well as philosophical essays, news, and politics are read aloud. In the past, this tradition helped to make cigar factory workers among its most politically aware and rebellious citizens.

Mountain life

The tropical rain forest which covered most of Cuba when the Spanish arrived began to disappear when the first Spanish farming communities were established. Then, when the sugar industry developed, the forest was cleared from nearly all the fertile land in Cuba, so that now it only covers the most remote and mountainous parts of the island.

The tropical rain forest is very dense, and very difficult to walk through. The people who live in the mountains, growing coffee and various fruits and vegetables on a small scale, have been isolated form the outside world. Electricity has still not reached many parts, so for many people the only daily contact and news from outside comes from battery-operated radios.

However, in recent years, a lot has changed. The building of new roads has made an enormous difference in the lives of people living in isolated areas. In the past, farmers would sometimes face ruin only because they did not have transportation to take their produce to the market. A sick child would have little chance of reaching a doctor since the distances would be impossible to travel. Although many new roads have been built, cars are quite rare. The horse and cart is still commonly used, although buses and tractors often provide an alternative.

When the government decided that health care and education should be available to all Cubans, they wanted even families living in the most

Horses still do a lot of work in the Cuban countryside, transporting people and their crops. In many ways, they are better than cars since they can travel more easily on the dirt roads and they do not need gas or spare parts, both of which are expensive and difficult to find.

isolated mountain communities to be included. So now country children are provided with transportation to school, accessible new hospitals, and doctors for all.

Cooperatives

Farmers who have for generations run their own little farm on their own are being encouraged to group with their neighbors, to form cooperative farms. By doing this, they can share the use of tractors and transportation to take their produce to their customers. Improved farming methods can be learned by sharing information, and by contact between the cooperative and the agricultural research institutes. The government encourages farmers by giving grants and loans to cooperatives. Farmers can even get government help to build new villages with electricity.

7   City Life

Young country people still move to the city in great numbers, even though the government steps in to help farmers in need. So large cities, such as Havana, the capital, are very crowded. Havana, in the west, is by far the largest of Cuba's main cities. The metropolitan area population of Havana is about two million, approximately 20 percent of the whole Cuban population. The next largest city is Santiago de Cuba in the east, with nearly 400,000 inhabitants.

Homes and places

The older buildings in the cities show the influence of the Spanish, who built them. The style is known as the baroque style, with ornate ironwork adorning the windows and verandas. This style can be seen in *Habana Vieja*, Old Havana, Havana's old colonial district, and in the centers of Santiago and the other cities.

> **Vedado**
> Vedado is Havana's main commercial center. This area is full of twentieth-century office buildings, hotels, and apartments. The most famous hotel just before the revolution was the Havana Hilton, which was completed in 1958. This is still a center for tourists who arrive in Cuba but it is now called the Havana Libre. Vedado is Havana's "downtown" area, with the wide main street leading down to the sea front, La Rampa, where young people go to stroll in the evenings to show off their smart clothes, before going to the nightclubs.

The older houses in Havana and other larger towns are very beautiful, with their elaborate stucco decoration and wrought iron balconies. Over the years many had become very run down but now they are being restored with the help of a grant from UNESCO.

The Old Havana streets are narrow, and although the buildings are grand, many are in need of repairs. This is because, as Havana grew, the richer inhabitants left the old city to move into the new suburbs, where they had large mansions built. The old district was left for the poor to live in. Since the rents were high, whole families had to live in single rooms. They had no money to maintain the buildings, and their landlords had no reason to spend their money on repairs either, because of the great demand for available housing.

A big program to improve the housing in Old Havana has begun, with the help of United Nations funds. The buildings are considered to be worth preserving, so the restoration is done with great care. The job is a big one, because of the many years of neglect, and there are still many homes with no basic facilities, such as a clean water supply.

The districts where the wealthy built their new mansions are only a short walk from the shanty towns where the new migrants from the countryside built their shacks. While the rich areas boasted grand architecture with sweeping lawns and well-kept flowerbeds, the poor areas had wooden shacks crammed together along dirt tracks and paths.

Overcrowding
Today, the rich have either left Cuba or have learned to accept a more modest lifestyle. Although some still live in their grand houses, they do not have the teams of servants they used to have, and can no longer buy all the luxury foreign-made goods that their money could once purchase.

Many of the shanty towns with the worst conditions have now been cleared, and replaced by new apartment buildings around the outskirts of the large towns. However, more people still arrive in Havana each year, attracted by the opportunities offered by city life. So although

This view across Havana shows the elegant, but crumbling, old town as well as the newer parts of the city. Before the revolution the government encouraged the building of skyscrapers as hotels and offices. However, these buildings were often surrounded by buildings which were very overcrowded and becoming slums.

many new homes have been built, the problem of overcrowding has not been resolved. Much effort is still spent trying to improve the situation. More houses, refurbishing of older homes, water, and power lines are needed. The government cannot afford to do all these things, so some of the work is done by volunteer "brigades." Materials are provided to help those who are able to fix up their own homes.

Cars and buses

One of the first things that might strike a visitor to a Cuban city is that there are relatively few cars on the roads. Unlike most major cities of the world, there is no need for parking meters. Cubans may complain about rush-hour traffic jams, but they are minor delays compared with those in cities in other countries. There are few cars because it is very difficult to get a car in Cuba. Most of the available cars date from 1959 or are imported from the Soviet Union or Eastern Europe. A few Japanese cars are now appearing on the streets, a sign that new trading links are being made.

In order to become the proud owner of a car, a Cuban has to earn it through exceptional work or contributions to society, or try to buy an old one from another person. The trouble with trying to buy a car is that there are so few for sale. When they are sold, they can cost more than a whole year's income. The old cars are mainly very heavy, grand old American cars, such as Chevrolets, Buicks, Fords, and Cadillacs. They consume a lot of gas, and parts are hard to find.

Since there are so few cars, most Cuban city dwellers travel by public transportation. The bus

Cars are very difficult to acquire in Cuba and they are usually very expensive. The most popular models are the large, old American cars. These are lovingly cared for by anybody lucky enough to acquire one. However, spare parts for any vehicle, even if much more recent, are hard to find.

fares are cheap, and the buses run throughout the day and night, but become very crowded in peak times. In the damp heat of the Cuban afternoon, the journey from work in these crowded buses can be very exhausting. Breakdowns make the problem worse. When the overcrowded buses breakdown, it can be difficult to get them repaired because of shortages of spare parts.

Frustrations
However, the Cubans usually accept these problems with little complaint. They are used to such inconveniences, because mechanical breakdowns and shortages are a common part of their life. These problems are caused in part by the fact that a lot of equipment is imported from abroad, so that reserve equipment is hard to get. It is also costly, and sometimes beyond the means of the Cuban economy. As there is not enough trade with foreign countries, there is a lack of foreign currency to buy imported goods. These problems are understood by everyone. There is little that anyone can do about them, except work hard to earn more foreign currency and help to develop the Cuban economy.

However, Cubans recognize that some of the difficulties are not only the result of technical problems. Many Cubans express their dissatisfaction with inefficient administrators or incompetent factory managers.

The administrators' performance is very important in Cuba, because all industry is owned and controlled by the central government. The government planners decide what should be produced and how it should be made. The advantage of central control is that production is not just for profit, but for the needs of the whole country. The problem is that when the economy changed to this system, many people had to become administrators with little training.

The problems of wasteful, poor quality and slow production due to poor factory management or bad attitudes of the workers are also hotly debated by Cubans. The expected standards of hard work and enthusiasm are very high, and the frustrations of not being able to find spare parts can be great. Cubans know well that there are no easy solutions, but they also know that day-to-day problems can be very exhausting, and they must keep trying in order to make progress.

Shopping
For a visitor from another country Cuban shops seem strange. There are no brightly colored advertisements urging people to buy goods. Window displays are dull because little attempt is made to entice shoppers to come in and buy.

The basic needs of food and essential clothing are available as a right to all Cubans. Each Cuban citizen receives a ration for food and clothes that they can use to buy goods at very cheap prices. The ration system ensures that no children go barefoot and all people have enough food. Only the basic foods are available on rations, such as the rice and beans that are the main food of Cubans, eggs, bread, milk, and some meat. Since there are no competing products or attempts to increase sales, items are wrapped in dull, plain paper with just a simple description of what the packages contain.

Shops in Cuba do not have large advertising signs outside, so they are often quite difficult to spot! However, there is usually a long line of people waiting patiently for service, which helps to identify the shops.

Sometimes the service in Cuban shops is slow, and shoppers have to wait for a long time. This can make shopping very tiring. Cubans have developed a system of waiting without staying in line. When people arrive, you can hear them say "*El ultimo?*" which means "the last one?" The person who arrived last will say so, and the new person can then try to find a place to sit in the shade, knowing that their place is reserved.

Shortages

Although basic food is available for everyone, it makes a very boring diet. While it is easy for people to find clothes to wear, it is not at all easy to find clothes which they wish to wear. As Cuba is a poor country, which is only starting to build up its own industry under difficult circumstances, there are many shortages. For example, meat is greatly valued. Despite the increase in the supply of meat in recent years, people still want more. As a result, when the word spreads that meat can be bought at a certain shop, shoppers will go there to wait immediately. The same is true of other items that are hard to find.

Gradually, the Cuban economy will be able to produce more and more goods, but in the meantime people's expectations and appetite for more and better goods always seems to reach beyond what is available.

Going out
In the warm tropical evenings, "going out" does not have to mean going to any place in particular. Groups of friends gather on street corners to chat

The Club Tropicana is one of the few nightclubs that still survives from before the revolution. The costumes of the Tropicana dancers still show the influence of the ideas of glamour in the U.S. of the 1950s.

and listen to music. Most streets are safe places for children to play while their parents talk because there are so few cars. One way to get different kinds of food is to go out to a cafe or restaurant. This has become more and more popular in recent years. Havana boasts Italian, Spanish, Polynesian, Chinese, and French restaurants, as well as those selling traditional Cuban food. The cheaper cafes are always busy, serving quick, simple snacks, and the ice cream parlors have the longest waiting lines of all.

In the evenings, if there are no house parties or street parties to go to in the neighborhood, those who want to dance can go to discotheques or cabarets, where live bands play. The biggest cabaret show of all is in the Tropicana night club in Havana, where one can enjoy modern and traditional Cuban music and dance. There are movies and plays, concerts and operas open throughout the year, and the ticket prices are kept low so that they are accessible to all.

8 Trade and Development

Sugar is the lifeblood of the Cuban economy, but it is also its poison. If the sugar harvest is good and the price is high, Cubans can expect an increase in their standard of living, but if the harvest fails or the price falls, they can expect shortages and difficulties. If Cuba continues to rely on sugar, this cycle of good years and bad years will continue. As more and more sugar has been produced in the world, its price has drifted downward. It is clear that the only way to increase the standard of living permanently is to develop the economy so that Cuba can make a wider range of goods and use new technologies.

The development problem
Building a new economy after so many years of dependence on sugar presented a huge development problem. In order to produce goods, Cuba needed to invest in new equipment and factories. In order to invest, it was necessary to buy equipment from abroad which was not yet produced in Cuba. In order to pay for that machinery, Cuba had to export something and all it had to export was sugar. In order to export enough, Cuba had to produce and export more sugar. In order to export more sugar, workers and machinery had to be switched from producing other goods to producing sugar. This problem proved a difficult one, and it is one which Cuba is still trying to solve.

Finding solutions

For many years, the economic planners have tried to get around these problems in different ways. They have tried to reduce the amount of money spent on other things, such as consumer goods and luxuries, so that the money can be saved to build new industries. At times, the planners have arranged for Cuba to borrow money from overseas lenders, which will have to be paid back in the future. They have also tried to make agreements with other sugar exporters to try to limit total sugar production, so that the price stops falling. Most of all, they have had to rely on the energy and determination of the workers.

New industries

Slowly and with great effort, Cuba has succeeded in building its economy. New factories have been built to make steel, which can then be used to make the machines that are needed to make other products. To build new houses, schools, and hospitals the building materials first have to be available so new cement works and other factories making building materials have developed all over Cuba.

As well as increasing the capital goods industries, those that provide materials for industry and building, the Cubans' household needs must be met. When trade with the U.S. ceased in 1961 Cubans lost their main supplier of goods. Cubans had to learn how to make the clothes, shoes, and household appliances that used to be imported. In addition, the equipment used for sports, particularly baseball, Cuba's favorite sport, had all been imported from the

After Cubans broke off relations with the U.S., they discovered they had no suppliers of equipment for their favorite sport—baseball! Factories were set up quickly to make balls and bats and there is now a thriving industry.

U.S. Now Cuba makes its own baseball bats, balls, and gloves, as well as footballs, boxing gloves, and racing canoes.

The food problem

With most of the agricultural land devoted to the production of sugar and tobacco for export, a lot of food had been imported from the U.S. All the vegetables eaten in Havana had come from Florida, and even when Cuba did produce some vegetables, like tomatoes, they were exported fresh in exchange for canned tomatoes. So in the early years after the revolution, Cuba faced food shortages, and further danger of hunger loomed. To make sure that the meager supply of food was shared so that no one starved, a ration system had to be introduced. Instead of meat, people had to make do with eggs. The system was effective in solving the problem of starvation, but after over ten years of eating eggs at nearly every meal, Cubans were sick of the sight of them. Even now, many Cubans are still egg-haters!

A varied diet

With the development of the cattle- and pig-farming industries, the situation has improved. There has been a great deal of research into better livestock breeding and farming methods suitable for the Cuban climate and soil, and the livestock population has multiplied. To add to the variety of the Cuban diet, the fishing industry has also been greatly expanded. The fishing fleet is now equipped to take advantage of the riches of the seas surrounding the island.

Cuba needed to grow different crops so that it was not so dependent on imported food. Now Cuba produces nearly 800,000 tons of citrus fruits. This orchard of newly planted orange trees is being hoed with minitractors to prevent the weeds from growing between the trees and using up the available water.

The biggest logistical problem involving food in Cuba is the challenge of getting a varied diet to the people in the cities, and especially to the two million inhabitants of Havana. In the countryside, fresh fruit and vegetables are usually available, but the difficulty is getting them to the city people while they are still fresh, and in storing food so that there is a good variety all year round. Part of the solution lies in developing canning and processing plants, as well as developing refrigerated transportation.

Energy and conservation

On posters in Cuban streets, people are asked to *ahorra*, that is, to save, for the good of the country. They are asked to save fuel, electricity, water, paper, bottles, and metal.

Cuba has hardly any oil or other fuels that can be found underground. Most of its oil is imported

Ahorra, "to save," is the Cuban solution to the conservation problem. The recycling of waste paper, scrap metal, and used bottles in Cuba is very impressive. Local community organizations, schools, hospitals, and offices organize the collection of these materials, which are sent to the local recycling plants. The paper is turned into pulp and made into paper again. The bottles are cleaned, sorted, and sent back to the dairies, or medicine factories that they came from. The metal is sorted and crushed, to be melted down and used again. Cuba is doing this to save money, but can also boast that it is helping to preserve the Earth's natural resources, instead of wasting them.

These "donkeys" are pumping oil from one of Cuba's few oil sources. Cuba manages to produce only 7 million barrels of its own oil, which means it is very dependent on imported oil.

from the Soviet Union for a cheap price. Any oil that Cuba does not use can be sold on the world market, at a price higher than the price at which Cuba buys it. Therefore, the more oil saved, the more can be exported, bringing valuable foreign earnings. In the future, it is hoped that energy can be produced in Cuba. A nuclear power plant has been built, and methods of using sugar by-products for fuel are being developed. Research into solar power is also underway.

Although a lot of rain water falls on Cuba, many people still do not have a piped water supply and many crops are still lost when there is a drought. Huge dams and reservoirs are being built, and irrigation systems and new pipes are being laid, but all this takes time and expensive materials. The only solution is ahorra.

Selling abroad

As well as finding new ways to make the things it used to buy, Cuba has to find new products to sell. A whole new range of products have been added to the traditional exports of sugar, rum, tobacco, cigars, and metals such as nickel.

Many of the new exports come from the industries that were developed to meet the needs of Cuba's own economy and society. Steel, cement, and other building materials made from recycling and from sugar by-products are now sold abroad. The efforts to build up education and culture have developed a publishing and printing industry that supplies books to other nations. The health industry has produced goods for export as researchers have invented new medical equipment and discovered new medicines. Even

Cubans are very proud of their latest development in high technology. It is a small machine for detecting the presence of the AIDS virus in blood at an early stage. There is a great deal of international interest in the machine.

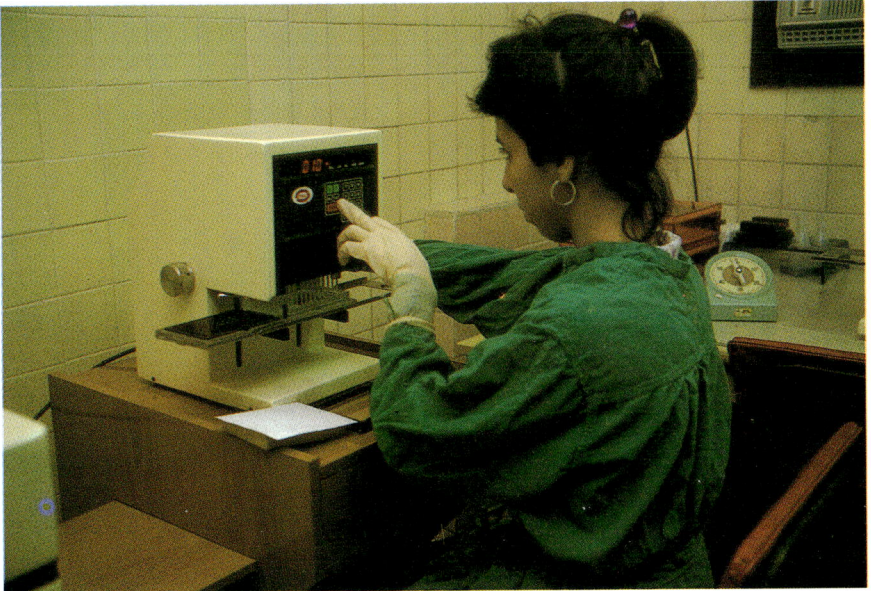

food is now exported, as citrus fruits and some of the tropical fruits find new markets, and the fishing fleet takes its catch to foreign ports.

Looking for customers

The hostility between Cuba and the U.S. has meant that Cuba has lost not only the U.S. market, but also relations have become difficult between Cuba and other countries, especially in Latin America. As many of these countries depend on the U.S. for trade and political support, they will not attempt to counter the U.S. When the U.S. broke diplomatic relations with Cuba, all the other Latin American countries apart from Mexico complied with the U.S.

To make up for these lost markets, Cuba has had to look for other partners farther away, in Europe, Africa, and the Far East. Also, some countries in Europe have increased trade with Cuba, notably Spain and the Scandinavian countries. Canada has also continued to build up trade. Gradually, over the past few decades, Cuba has been restoring diplomatic and trading links with the other countries of Central and South America.

Trading with the Soviets and Eastern Europe

Today, Cuba's most important partners are the Soviet Union and the Eastern European countries. They account for about 80 percent of all Cuba's trade. Ever since the Soviet Union agreed to buy Cuban sugar, Cuba has enjoyed strong trading links on very good terms with the Soviet Union and its allies. When Cuba does not have enough money to buy essential imports, it can

Cuba is trying very hard to expand the variety of industries it has. New industrial areas are being developed outside some towns. This large factory is now surrounded by other industrial units and is served by a new four-lane highway.

arrange barter deals with its Eastern European friends. This means that it can have the imports in exchange for goods such as sugar or fruits, instead of money. Trading with the Soviet Union, which is on the other side of the world, is not as easy as it was to trade with Cuba's neighbor, the U.S. With such a large distance to transport goods, it is difficult not to lose money on imports. Deliveries take a long time, and can be unreliable. A further problem is that the Soviet Union uses different measurements for machine parts than the U.S. Any part ordered by Cuba has to be specially made-to-measure. Trade with the Soviets and Eastern Europe have been the lifeline for Cuba, but due to the sweeping changes in Europe, future trade relations are uncertain.

Clear blue seas and white sands make miles of beaches that are a tourist's dream. For years, the Cubans had these beaches almost all to themselves, but now the tourists are beginning to return.

Bringing back the sunseekers

After the revolution, Cuba lost a source of income from North American tourists who could no longer come and visit, and tourism slumped altogether. As stability has returned and the economy is stronger, the tourist industry is being built up again. Like the other Caribbean islands, Cuba has a lot to offer tourists, with its magnificent beaches and sunshine all year round. For nature lovers, there are mountains and forests, and there are many beautiful and unspoiled towns and cities. All kinds of sports can be enjoyed and Cuba is an exciting place for music lovers. With all efforts being concentrated on improving facilities for Cubans, the tourists were a low priority for some years after the revolution. Then, a massive hotel-building program was undertaken, to make room for a quarter million tourists a year. Tourism is now set to become one of Cuba's main sources of the foreign currency needed for development.

9 The Future

Cuba is a land of young people. Over half of today's population was born after the revolution, which so dramatically changed the Cuban way of life. Many people left Cuba after the revolution, but those that remained are proud of what they have achieved in their country. They are also proud of their own unique culture and of their independence.

Today, in Cuba, the children are no longer half-starved and ragged. They are taller, sturdier, and healthier and able to enjoy a good education, even though the country remains poor.

High hopes and hard work

Today, the expectations of the young are very high, because of the achievements, which were beyond the wildest dreams of most Cubans before 1959. Having grown up in a period of rapid

progress, some are impatient for more improvements in the areas which still lag behind, such as fashion goods and stereo systems. Sometimes their parents watch this impatience and think of how hard they worked to make a better country for their children. The children are their hope for the future.

The big question mark

Young people in Cuba today have grown up with Castro as their political leader and the Communist party dominating political life. It has been a period of political stability despite the enormous challenges they have faced and changes that have happened.

As the new government grew older, its aging leaders kept their positions of power, so that younger people did not have much of a say in the important decisions. Attempts have been made to put that right, and the old men who have led Cuba for so long are politely retiring from their posts to allow others to take their places.

The biggest question mark in Cuba's future is how the political system will change when Castro no longer leads it. He has led the country through radical changes and he has no obvious successor to date.

Young people, not only in the Young Communist party but also in the students' organizations, are encouraged to discuss the problems that Cuba faces. Fidel Castro has often said that it is important to listen to the young and to give them power, as they are the most impatient, with the highest standards and lowest tolerance of failure.

Index

© Heinemann Children's Reference 1990
This edition originally published 1990 by
Heinemann Children's Reference, a division
of Heinemann Educational Books, Ltd.